Unbelievable Pictures and Facts About Bahrain

By: Olivia Greenwood

Introduction

Bahrain is a multilayered destination, filled with many wonderful and exciting things. Today we will be exploring the country of Bahrain in more detail.

Will you find any rivers in Bahrain?

Believe it or not, you will not find any rivers in the area. You will not find even one. The country is short on rainfall and the area is flat.

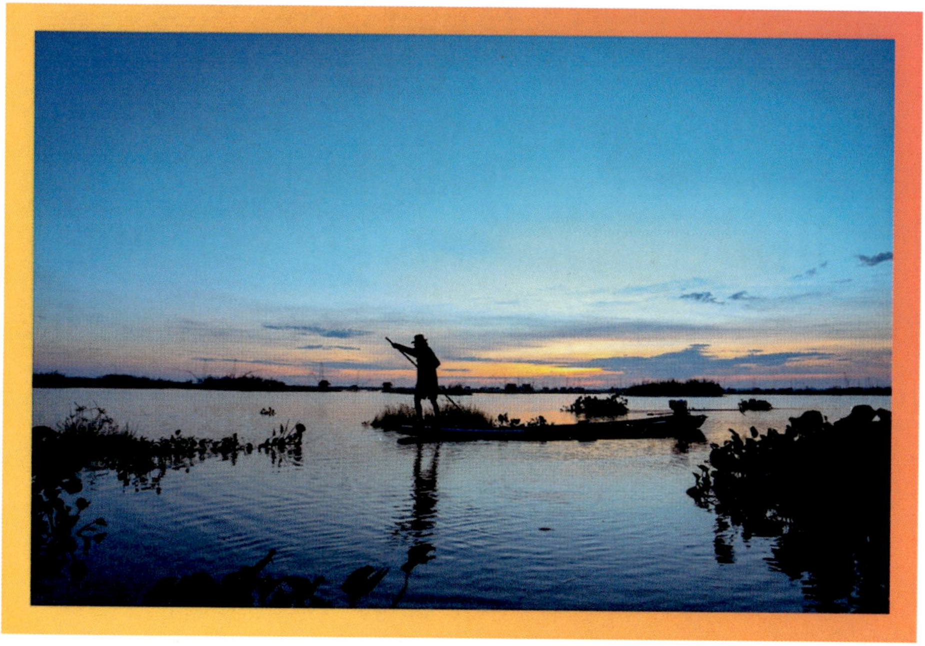

What languages do people speak in Bahrain?

If you go to Bahrain you will notice that the majority of people speak Arabic. People also have a tendency to speak English and Farsi.

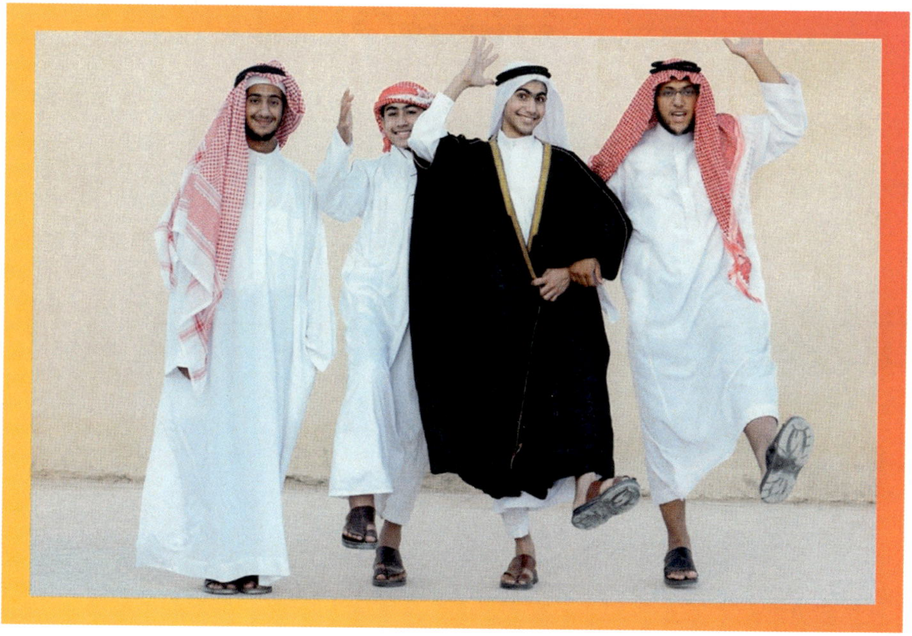

Is Bahrain a popular place for tourists to visit?

Bahrain is actually not a very popular place for tourists to visit.

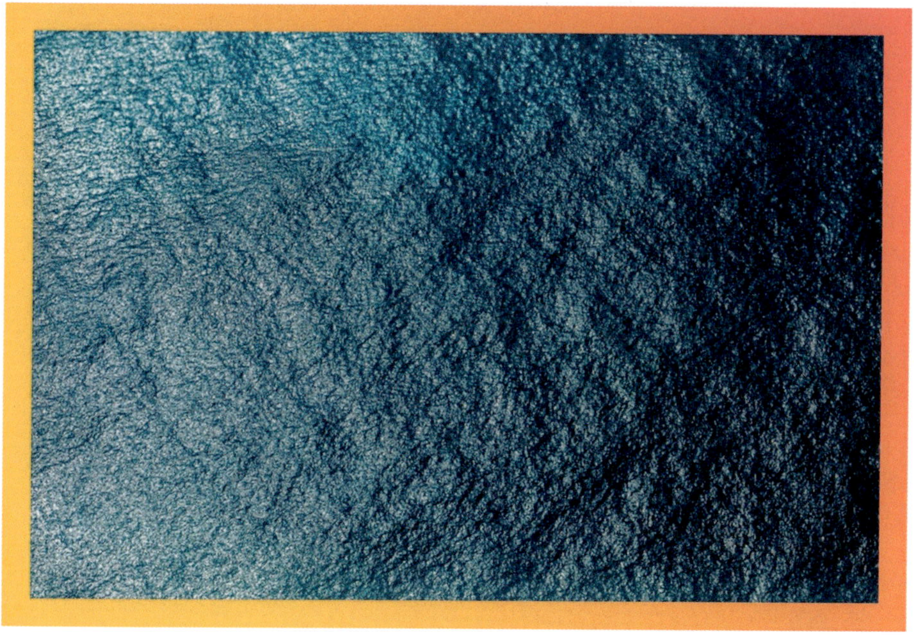

What year did the country become fully independent?

The country became fully independent in 1971.

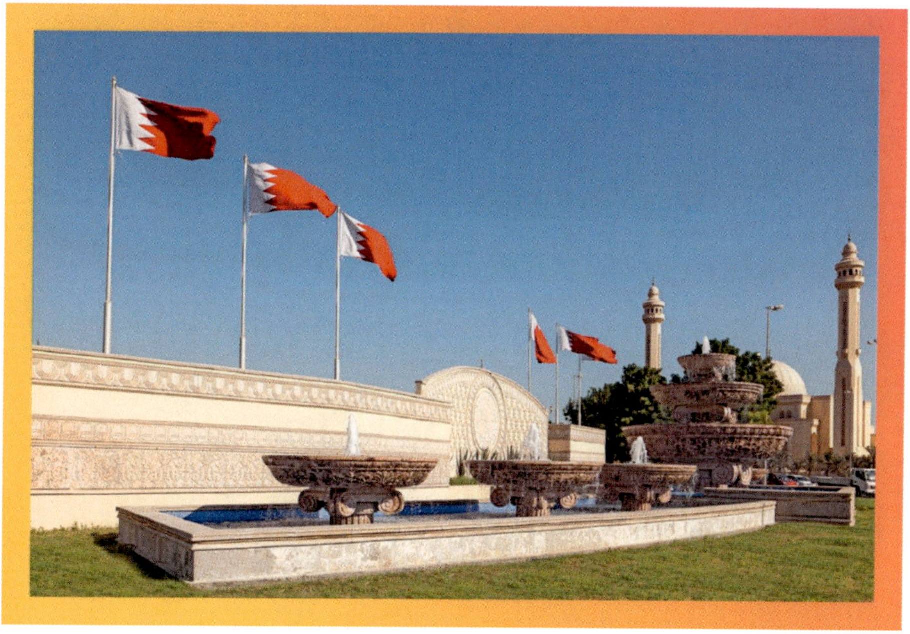

Which sport do people enjoy the most in the country?

They play a couple of different sports in Bahrain. However, the most popular sport which is played in the country is football.

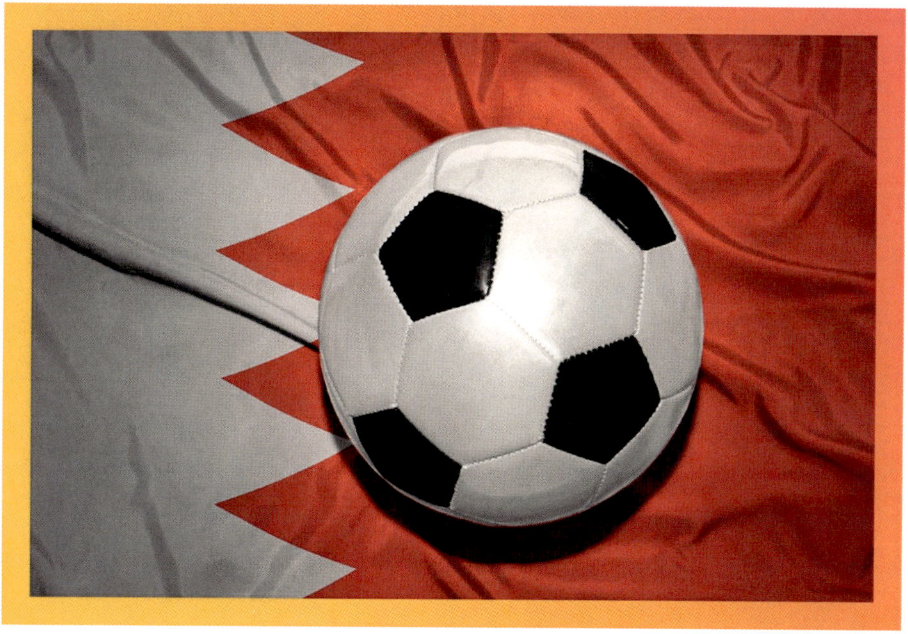

What does the country of Bahrain export the most?

Bahrain is actually a big exporter of many different goods. These goods consist of cars, iron, aluminum bars, and petroleum.

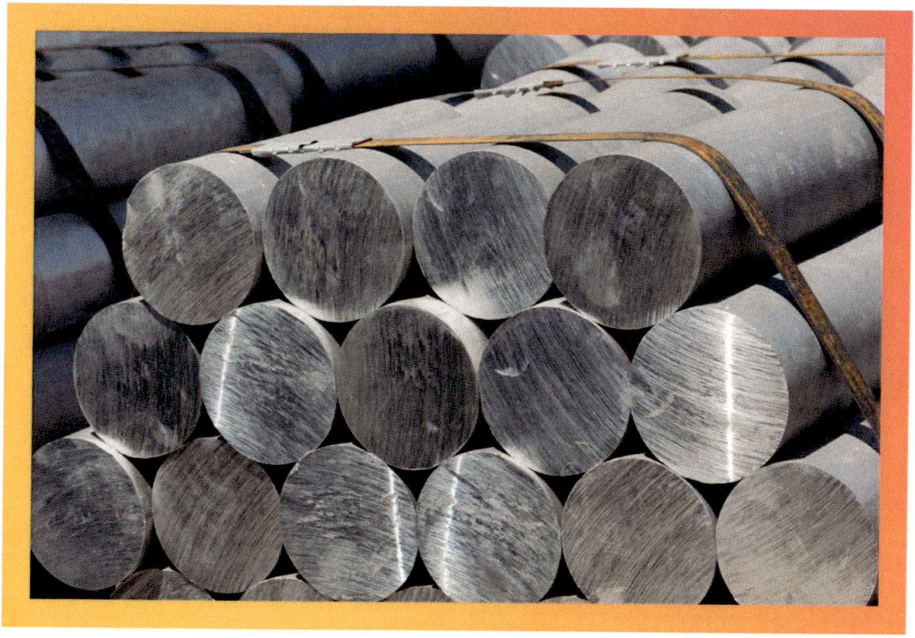

What religion is practiced the most in Bahrain?

The religion which is practiced the most in Bahrain is Islam.

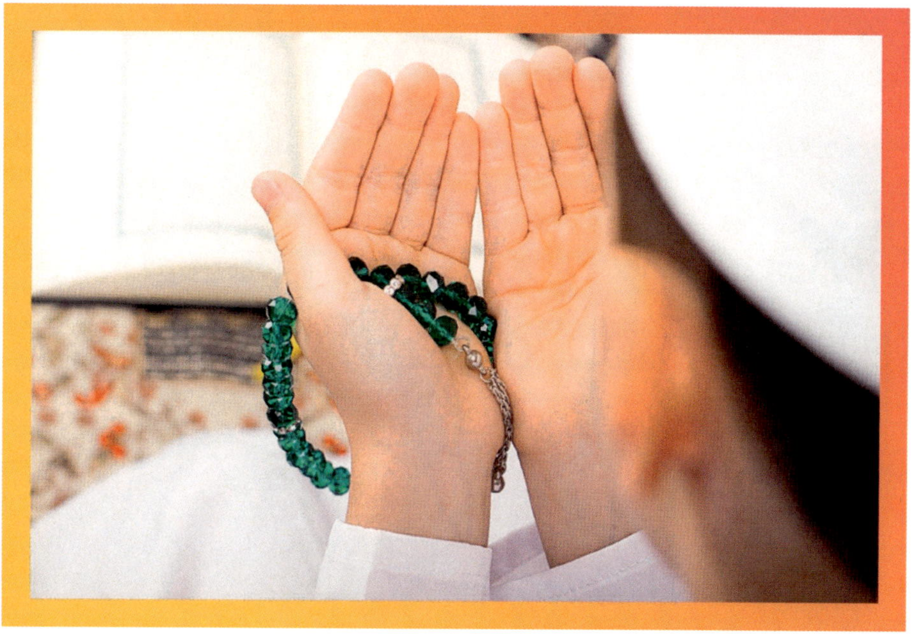

Are there any interesting museums in the country?

The answer is a big yes. There are a couple of really interesting museums to visit in Bahrain.

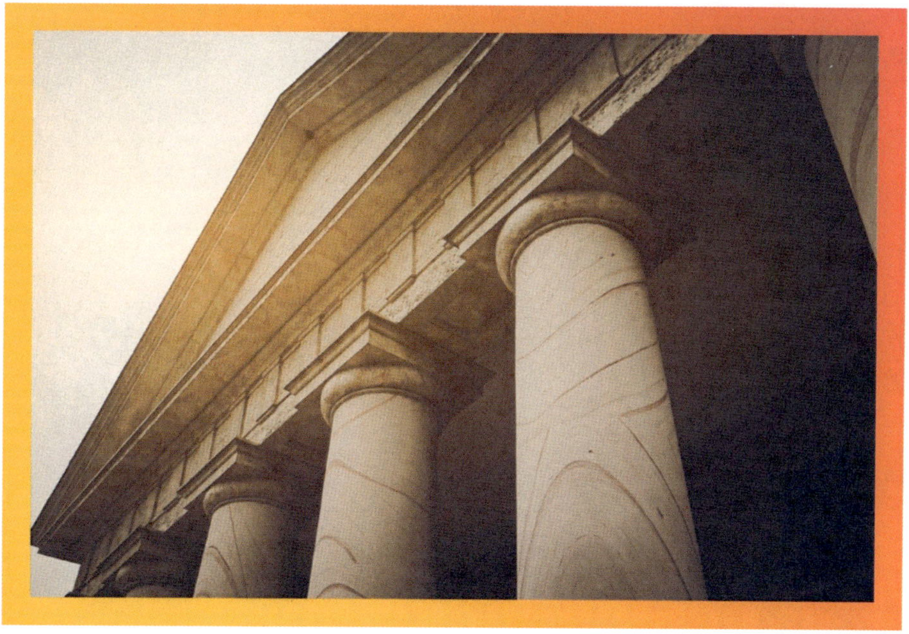

What type of food do they eat in Bahrain?

In Bahrain, they eat all sorts of interesting foods. One of the most famous dishes is called Machbous which is meat and rice.

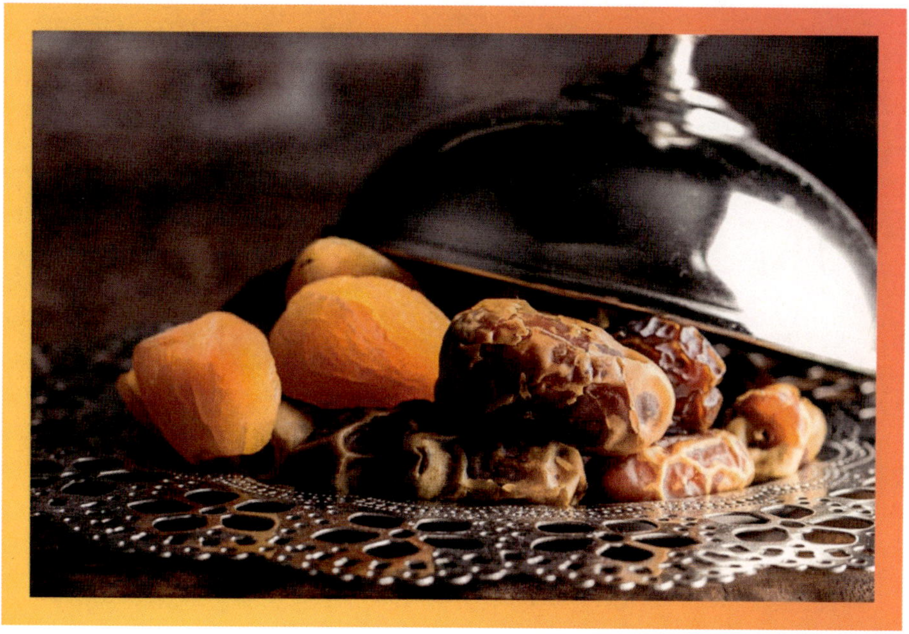

Does Bahrain have a particular national flower?

The answer is no. There has been no official national flower designated to Bahrain.

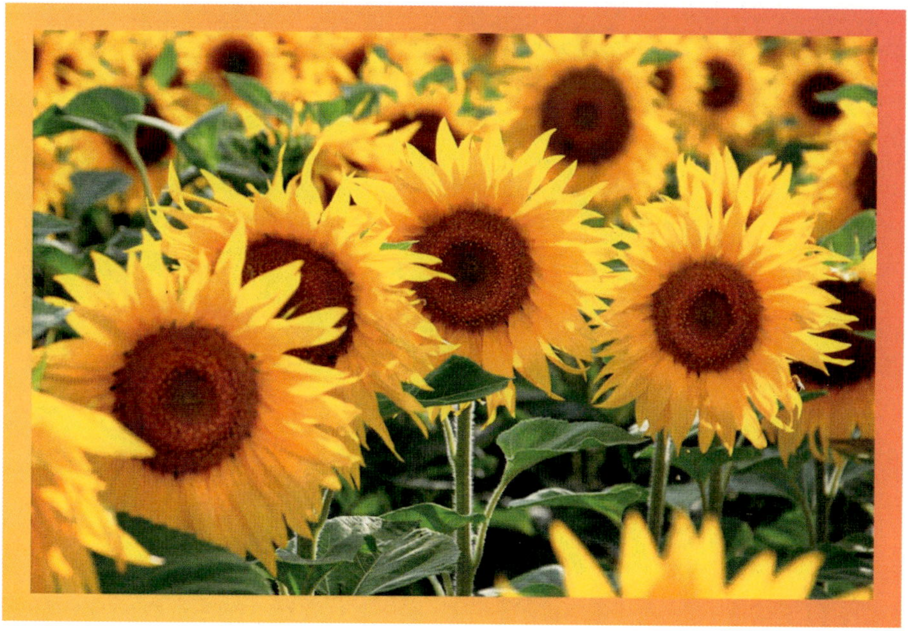

Which financial currency do they use in Bahrain?

If you ever plan on visiting Bahrain it may be useful for you to know which financial currency they use. The official financial currency used in Bahrain is the Bahraini Dinar.

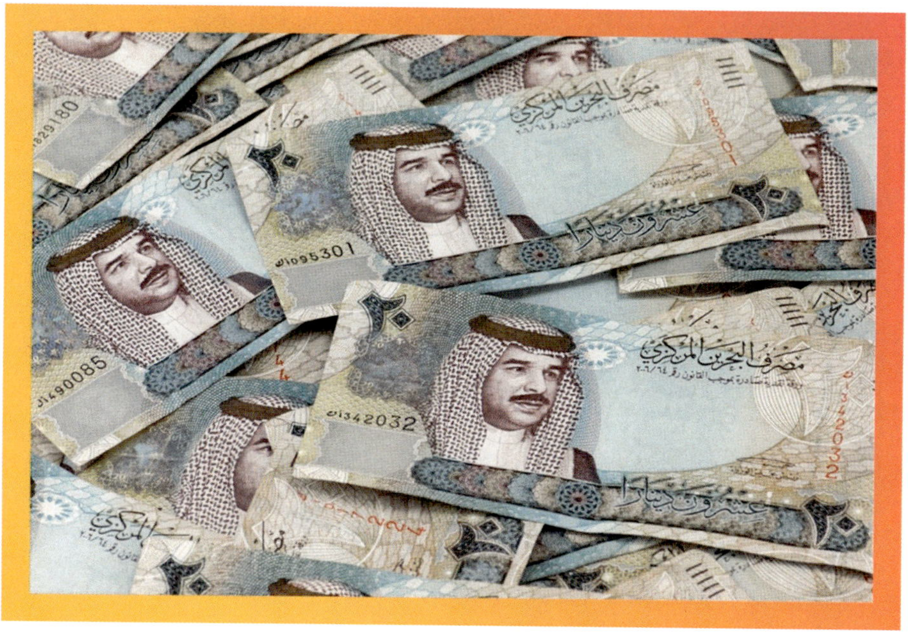

مصرف البحرين المركزي
عشرون دينارا
1342032
1095301

What is the population size in Bahrain?

In Bahrain, the current population size is around 2 million plus-minus. Most of the people living in Bahrain are between the ages of 14 and 65.

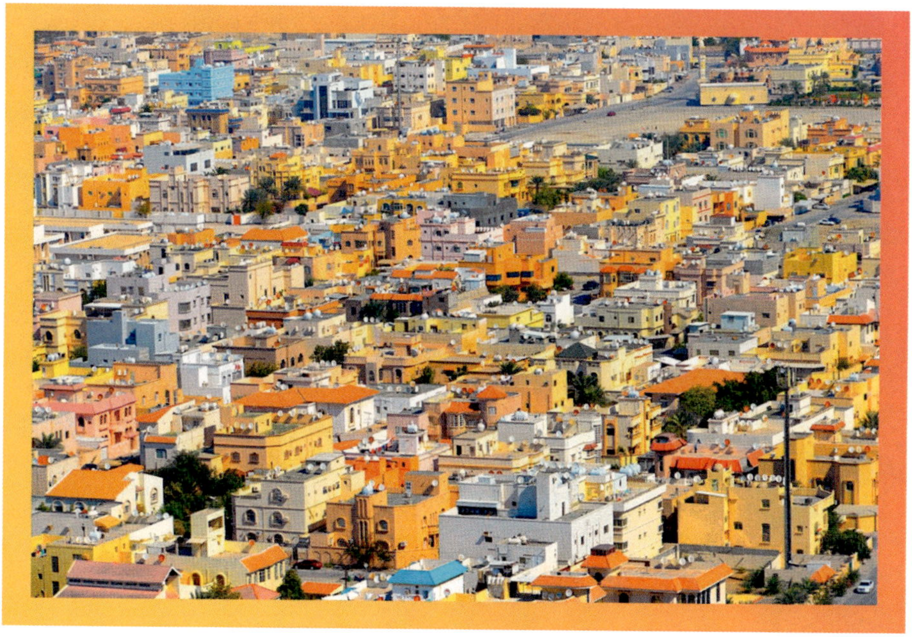

What does the capital city of the country go by?

The capital goes by the name of Manama. It is home to over 160,000 people.

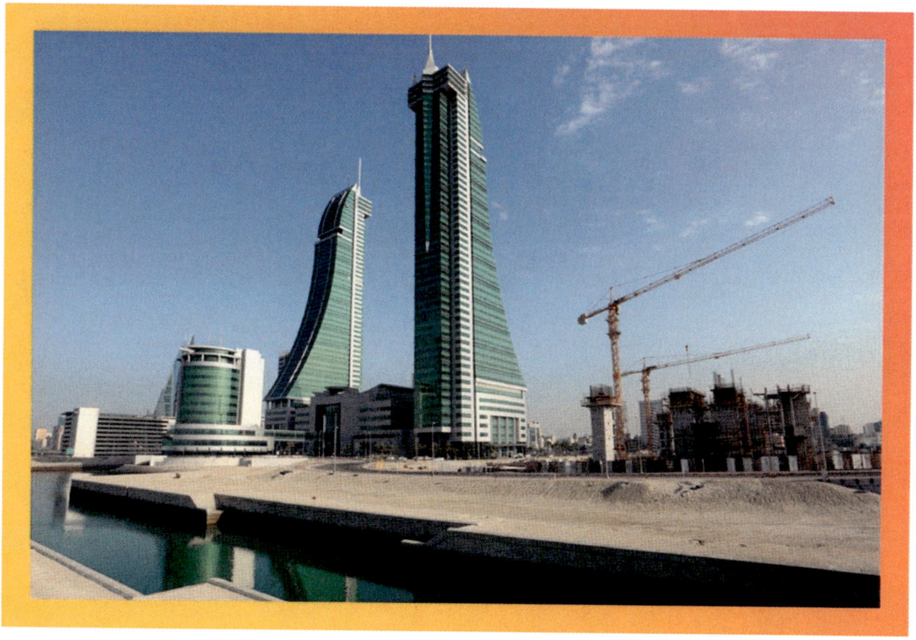

Is it cheap or expensive to buy things in Bahrain?

Although prices differ depending on what you buy, in general things are actually pretty expensive in Bahrain.

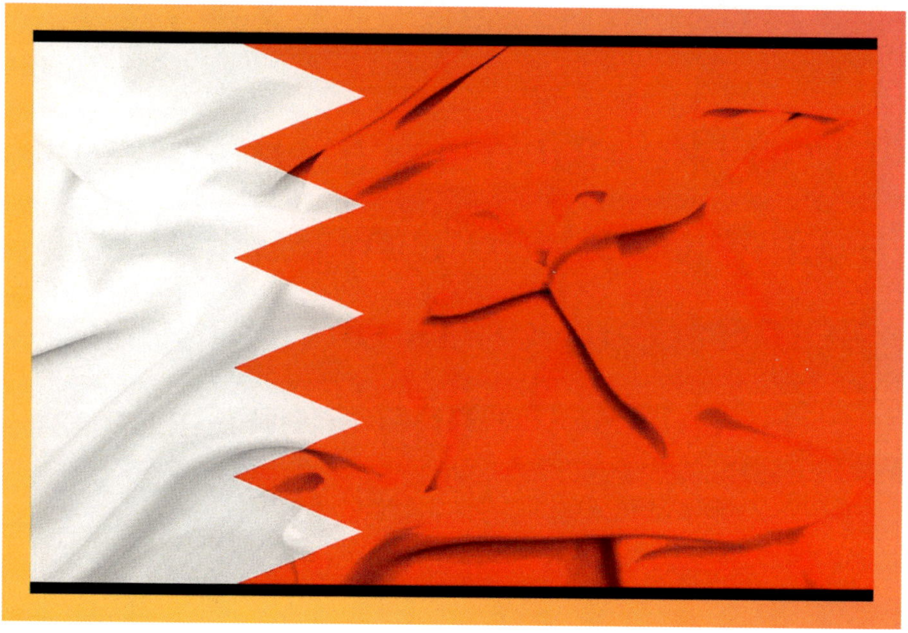

Will you find any animals in Bahrain?

If you like animals, then you will really love Bahrain. Bahrain is home to all kinds of wonderful and fascinating animals.

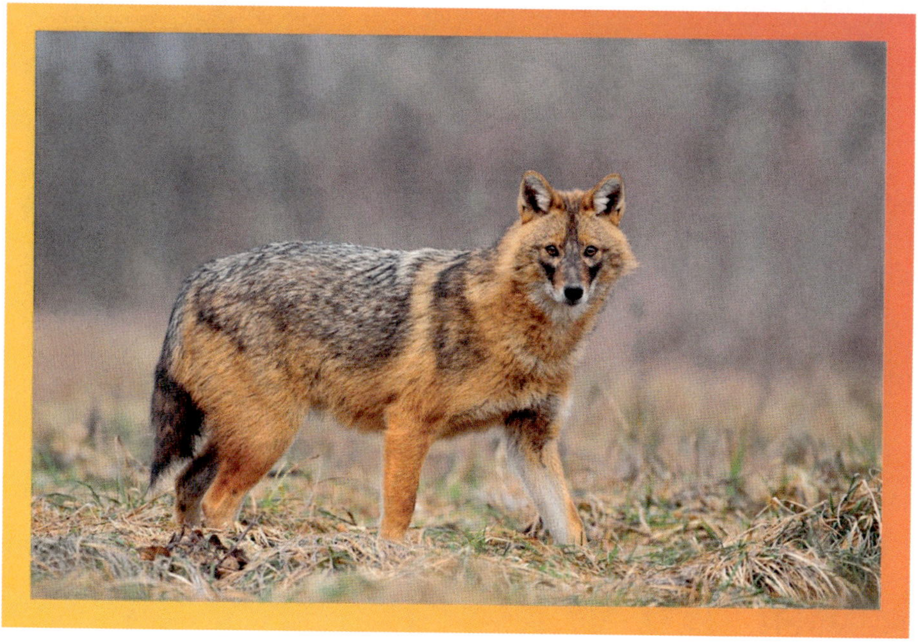

What type of weather do they experience in Bahrain?

Bahrain experiences four different seasons in the year. Although during the summer months it does have a tendency to get extremely hot. There is not much rainfall during the year.

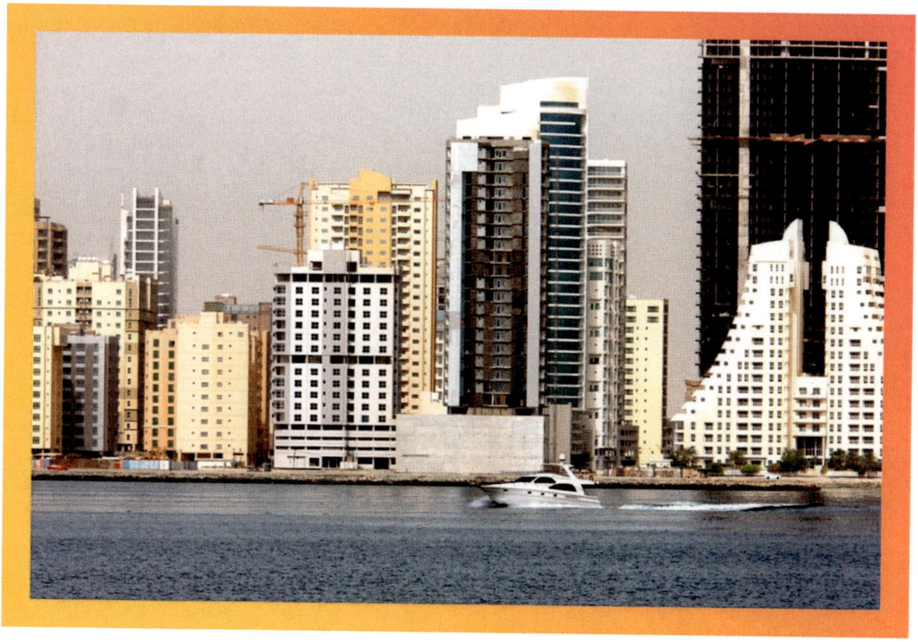

Is Bahrain a big or small country?

In comparison to many other countries, Bahrain is actually considered to be fairly small in terms of size.

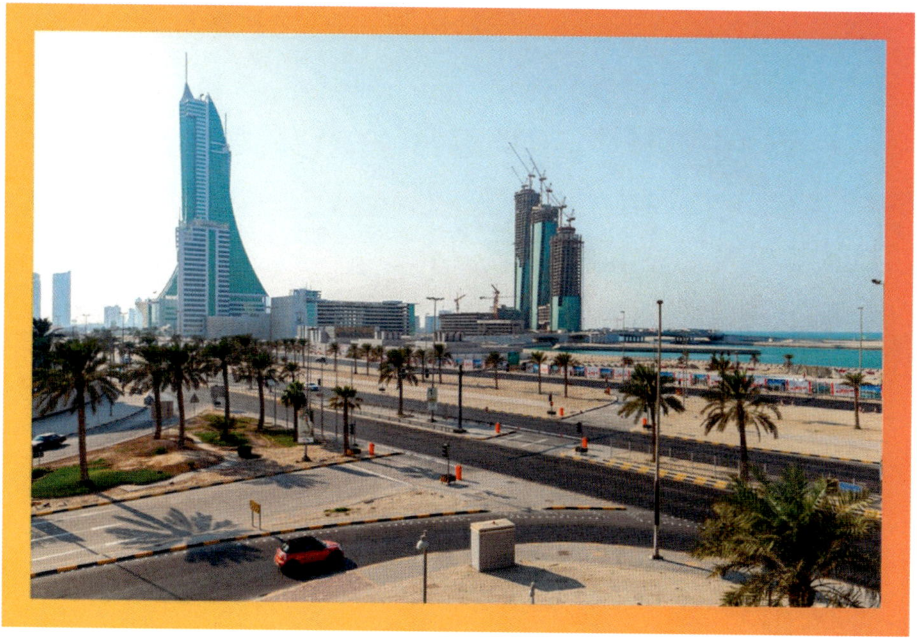

Is it safe to travel in Bahrain?

It is generally safe to travel in Bahrain. However, the crime rate has escalated in the last couple of years. If you are going to travel in Bahrain it is best to do so with a travel companion.

TURKMENISTAN
SYRIA
IRAQ
Baghdad
IRAN
An Najaf
Ahvaz
Yazd
Basra
Kuwait (Al Kuwayt)
Nafud
Kerman
Dasht-e Lut
Shiraz
Bushehr
SAUDI
Zahedan
Dhahran (Az Zahrān)
Manama (Al Manāmah)
BAHRAIN
Dubai
Bandar-e'Abbas
Medina
(Al Madinah)
QATAR
(Dubayy)
Doha
(Ad Dawhah)
Riyadh (Ar Riyad)
Abu Dhabi
ARABIA
U.A.E.
Gulf of Oman
Karachi
Jeddah (Jiddah)
Mecca (Makkah)
Muscat
Rub' al Khali

What type of landscape does the country have?

Bahrain is surrounded by islands. The landscape in Bahrain is truly magnificent.

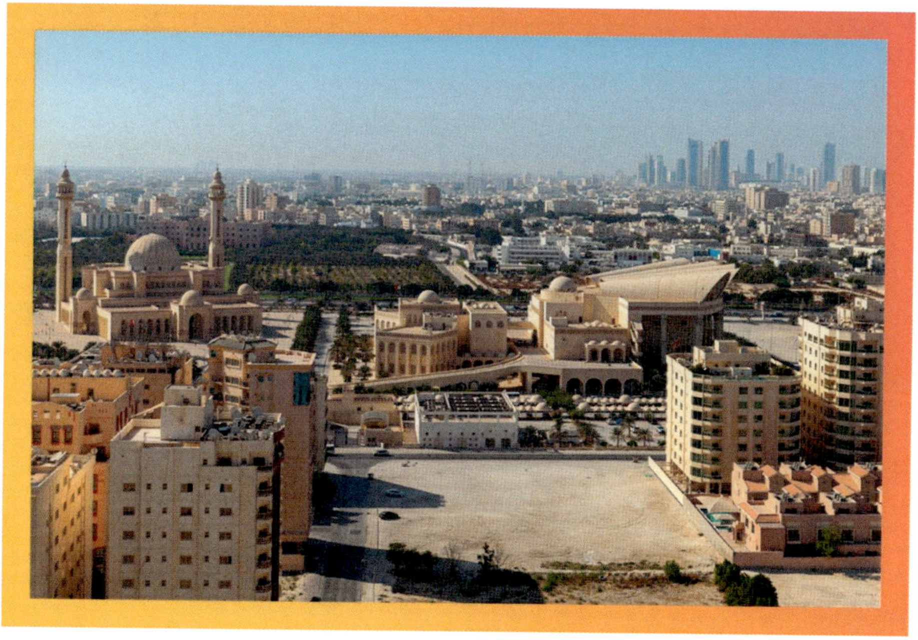

Where in the world is Bahrain situated?

Bahrain is actually a small island country, which is situated on the Persian Gulf.

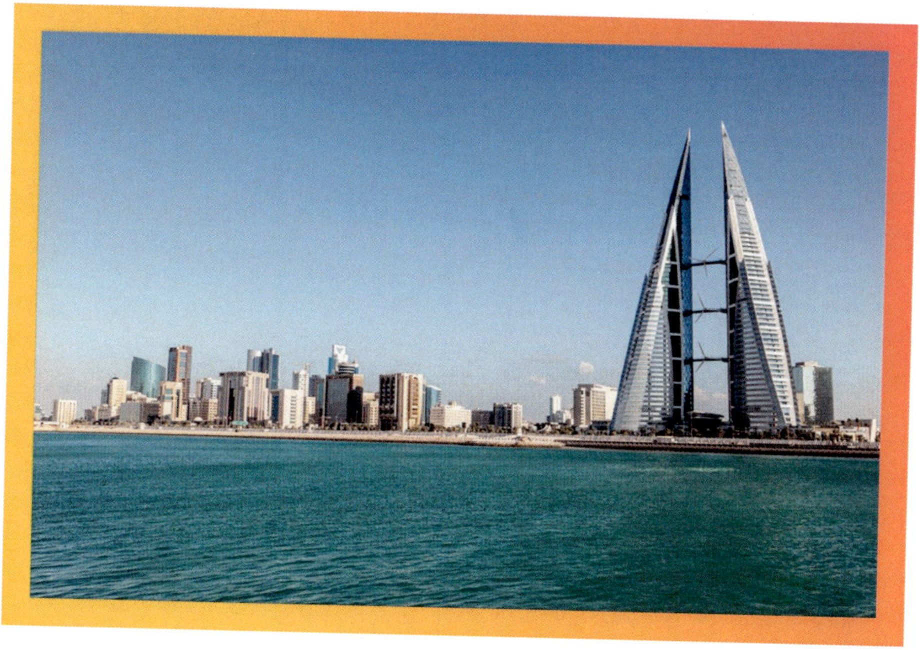

Made in the USA
Las Vegas, NV
30 June 2022